Sarah's Song

Written by Rosie J. Pova

Illustrated by Emma Allen

Sarah's Song
Text Copyright © 2017 by Rosie J. Pova
Artwork Copyright © 2017 by Emma Allen

Summary: Sarah wishes to find the perfect song to make her grandma better so they can enjoy music and dance together again – just like they used to.

Clear Fork Publishing
P.O. Box 870
102 S. Swenson
Stamford, Texas 79553
(325)773-5550
www.clearforkpublishing.com

Printed and Bound in the United States of America.
ISBN - 978-1-946101-35-8
LCN - 2017952989

www.clearforkpublishing.com

"In loving memory of my grandparents." – R.J.P.

"For Amelie, my little superstar." – E. A.

Sarah loved to sing and dance with Grandma.

"If you hold on to music, it'll always keep you going," Grandma had once told her.

Day after day, Sarah and Grandma moved to the beat as their voices joined together in song.

They spun and chanted through the living room.

They skipped and crooned at the park.

They coasted and caroled at the rink.

And they whistled and waded through fields of wild flowers.

Most of all, Sarah enjoyed their yearly tradition of performing at the Fall Festival.

But lately, Grandma became tired more and more, and she sang and danced less and less. She started using a cane.

If I find the right song, maybe I can get Grandma to sing and dance with me again, Sarah thought.

When Sarah sang an old song, Grandma clapped.

When she sang a new song, Grandma rocked.

When she sang a silly song, Grandma laughed.
Still, Grandma didn't sing along.

No matter how hard Sarah tried, Grandma's voice got weaker and her legs got wobblier.

"Grandma doesn't sing and dance with me anymore," Sarah told her mom. "And none of my songs make her better!"

"But she *feels* better when you sing and dance," her mom said. "Talk to her and you'll see."

Sarah ran over to Grandma.

"Grandma, if I find the perfect song,
will you please sing and dance along?"

"Oh, sweet Sarah, I wish I could," Grandma said. "I'm getting older and more tired. But watching *you* sing and dance brightens my day." Sarah sighed. *What if Grandma never sings and dances again?*

As the festival approached, Sarah's mom took her dress shopping. Sarah frowned at every choice.

"I don't even want to sing if I can't perform with Grandma," Sarah mumbled.

"She'd love to see you perform," her mom replied.

At home, Sarah's mom pulled out her sewing machine and fabrics to make a dress.

Sarah pulled out Grandma's old dress. "Mom, can you use *this* fabric?"

"Of course, I can. It's perfect."

Sarah hugged her new dress and twirled around Grandma.

"It looks beautiful on you," Grandma said. "Now, I'll be right there with you when you sing your song."

Which song should I sing? Sarah wondered.
She scribbled down her favorite songs and precious
memories. Then, she got an idea.

The next morning, Sarah rushed to see Grandma. "I know how I can start a new tradition!" she said. "I have a special surprise for you."

Grandma's eyes teared.
"I can't wait."

Sarah smiled at Grandma from the stage.
She took a deep breath and began singing
the song she'd created on her own.

♫♪Sparkle, sparkle little song
make my grandma dance along —
sing and swing and sway with me
like a birdie in the tree.
If I find the perfect song?
Can you dance and sing along? ♪♫♪

"Oh, Sarah!" Grandma said. "What a perfect song. You make my heart sing and dance. *That's* what counts."

Sarah beamed. "Then I'll keep singing and dancing for both of us, Grandma."

Rosie J. Pova is a children's author, poet, wife, and mother of three. Originally from Bulgaria, she now lives in Texas with her family.

Rosie loves music, but more than that, she loves to inspire children to dream big and follow their passions. No matter what kind of story she writes – funny, sweet or silly – Rosie hopes to move her readers and warm their hearts.

Rosie is also the author of *If I Weren't With You* (PB, Spork) and a humorous sci-fi middle grade novel, *Hailey Queen Pranking Makes Perfect: The Alien Encounter,* (MG, Spork).
Visit her at **www.rosiejpova.com**

Emma Allen is an Illustrator from Kent, England. Emma loves to recreate the magic of childhood with her paintbrush and illustrating whimsical scenes of children in the great outdoors, often in the company of animals, is a real passion. After working for years in acrylic Emma recently made the move to watercolor and has never looked back!

After studying at Central Saint Martin's College of Art and Design in London Emma went into a career in magazine production, and then changed direction after the birth of her daughter to follow her dream of becoming an Illustrator. Emma gained a Distinction in 'Illustrating Children's Books' from the London Art College and also achieved the 'Student of the Year' award.

Some of Emma's recent clients include Stoneworks Education Ltd, The Story Corner Ltd, Cocolivo, My Mother's Love and The Wild Tomorrow Fund. Emma is thrilled to be working with Clear Fork Publishing.

CPSIA information can be obtained
at www.ICGtesting.com
Printed in the USA
LVHW07*1608260318
571184LV00029B/508/P